Razzamajazz
Trumpet

The fun way to learn!

Razzamajazz Trumpet

The fun way to learn!

Sarah Watts

kevin
mayhew

kevin mayhew

First published in Great Britain in 2003 by Kevin Mayhew Ltd
Buxhall, Stowmarket, Suffolk IP14 3BW
Tel: +44 (0) 1449 737978 Fax: +44 (0) 1449 737834
E-mail: info@kevinmayhewltd.com

www.kevinmayhew.com

9 8 7 6 5 4 3 2 1

ISBN 978 1 84417 042 5
ISMN M 57024 179 8
Catalogue No. 3611736

Cover design: Rob Mortonson
Music setting: Donald Thomson
Proof reading: Tracy Cook

Printed and bound in Great Britain

Contents

Acknowledgement

Thank you to Alison Garbet, Marian Hellen, Nick Care and Kathy Gifford for their brass expertise.

A note from the composer

This is a fun book of jazzy pieces with a 'feel good' accompaniment to encourage you in the early stages of learning.

Although *Razzamajazz* is not a tutor, I hope you will enjoy learning the pieces and benefit from them.

SARAH WATTS

Introducing G

This is where it goes on the music

To play G do not press any valves

OH GEE!

NOTE USED - G

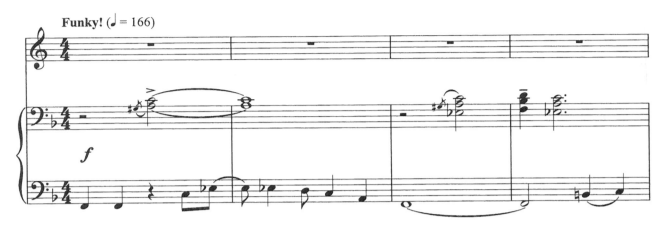

here's F

This is where it goes on the music

To play F
press the valve
coloured black

FLYING HIGH

NOTES USED - F, G

Light latin (♩ = 118)

8

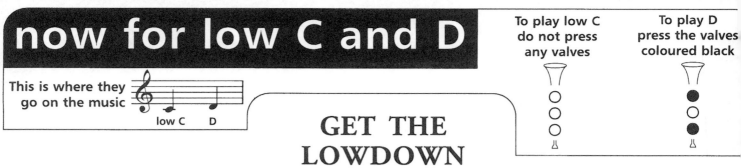

This is where it goes on the music

To play E press the valves coloured black

MR COOL

NOTES USED - low C, D, E, F

EVERY NOW
AND THEN

NOTES USED - E, F, G

SLEEPY SUBURB

NOTES USED - low C, D, E, F, G

MOVIE BUSTER

NOTES USED - low C, D, E, F, G

Driving (♩ = 150)

FANFARE FOR FUN

NOTES USED - low C, D, E, F, G

20

and next low B

This is where it goes on the music

To play low B press the valve coloured black

RHUBARB FOOL

NOTES USED - low B, low C, D, E, F, G

and on to A

This is where it goes on the music

To play A
press the valves
coloured black

TWENTY-FOUR SEVEN

By Sarah and Daniel

NOTES USED - low C, D, E, F, G, A

24

D.S. al Fine

D.S. al Fine

RAZZLE DAZZLE

NOTES USED - low C, D, E, F, G, A

here's F#

This is where it goes on the music

To play F#
press the valve
coloured black

SEPTEMBER BROWN

NOTES USED - low C, D, E, F#, A

Jazz waltz (♩ = 120)

28

29

now for B

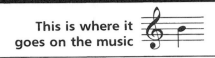

This is where it goes on the music

To play B press the valve coloured black

BATTERY SQUARE BOSSA

NOTES USED - low B, low C, D, E, F, G, A, B

Latin feel (♩ = 110)

and now C

This is where it goes on the music

To play C do not press any valves

FABBEROONIE

NOTES USED - low C, D, E, F, F♯, G, A, C

Rock feel (♩ = 130)

here's B♭

This is where it goes on the music

To play B♭ press the valve coloured black

TUBE TRAIN

NOTES USED - low B, low C, D, E, F♯, G, A, B♭, B

and finally low A

This is where it goes on the music

To play low A press the valves coloured black

BEBOP LONGBODY

*Owing to the nature of this book, I have used dotted rhythms.
More advanced players may play them with a 'Jazz quaver' feel.*